The Hamster Book

minibombo

First published in Great Britain 2017 by Walker Books Ltd, 87 Vauxhall Walk, London SE11 5HJ • Copyright © 2014 minibombo/TIWI s.r.l. • English language translation © 2017 Walker Books Ltd • First published 2014 by minibombo, Italy as *Il libro criceto* by Silvia Borando • Text & Illustration: Silvia Borando • Editing: Chiara Vignocchi • Graphic Design: Alberto Bonanni • Published in the English language by arrangement with minibombo, an imprint of TIWI s.r.l., Via Emilia San Pietro, 25, 42121 Reggio Emilia, Italy • minibombo is a trademark of TIWI s.r.l. © 2014 minibombo/TIWI s.r.l. The moral rights of the author have been asserted • This book has been typeset in Tisa Pro Regular and Medium • Printed in China

• British Library Cataloguing in Publication Data: a catalogue record for this book is available from the British Library • ISBN 978-1-4063-6772-0 • www.walker.co.uk • 10 9 8 7 6 5 4 3 2 1

MIX
Paper from responsible sources
FSC™ C020056

WALKER BOOKS
AND SUBSIDIARIES
LONDON · BOSTON · SYDNEY · AUCKLAND

Check out **www.minibombo.com** to find plenty of fun ideas for playing and creating – all inspired by this book!

I'll call my hamster:

. . . .

Zzz zzz

Look at your hamster...
She's fast asleep!
Come on, lazybones,
it's time to get up!
Can you help wake her?
Softly *tap tap tap* on her back
and then turn the page.

Squeak!

That woke her up!
Now she's ever so perky ...
and ever so scruffy!
Her fur is all in a ruffle.
Why don't you smooth it down
with your hand?

Much better.
Now she's ready to show you
something special –
her super, spinny-ball trick!
Cheer her on with
a wave and a whistle.
Shout her name and say,
"You can do it!"

Ooooooooooooh...

But wait, where's she going?
Come back, hamster –
we can't see your trick!

Oooooooooooh...

Oh no ... she's gone too far!

Quick, quick –
turn the page!

Well, not a *perfect* landing ...
but what an effort!
Go on, give her a nice big
round of applause.

After all that spinning,
your hamster is pretty hungry!
Use your fingers to feed her
some sunflower seeds.
Give her every single one.

Oh, my...
Her mouth is completely full!
Chew, hamster. Chew.
Give her a few seconds to
gulp them down,
and then turn the page.

Too soon – she's still chomping!
Let's wait a few more seconds.
Three ... two ... one...

Uh-oh. What has she done now?
What a mess!

Can you help clear it up?
Don't forget to use a tissue!

Good job – she's squeaky clean again!
But now she's pretty tired.
It's been quite a busy day, after all.
Wish her a good night
with a little tickle
on her tummy.

Then slowly, so very slowly,
turn the page.

Shhh!

She's asleep.
Good night, fuzzy furball.
Sleep tight.

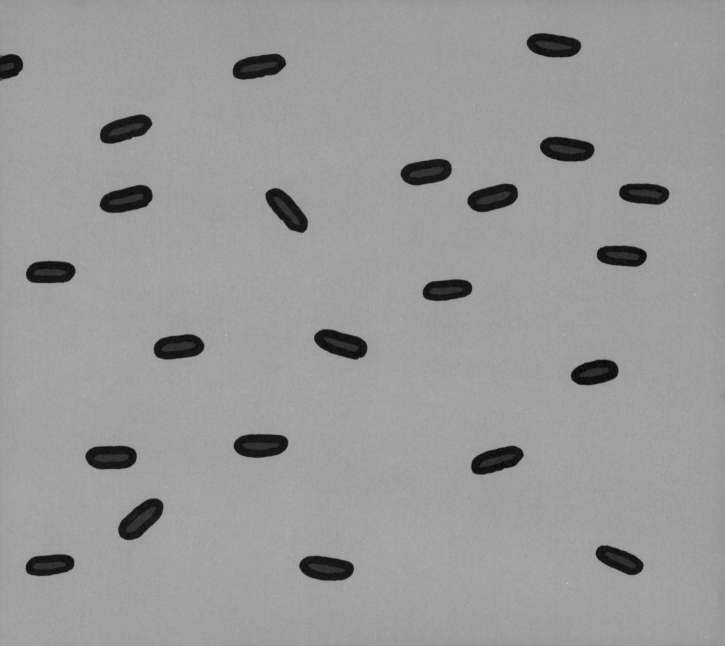